Hop to the Shop

T0318103

Written by Mary Roulston

Illustrated by Helen Flook

Collins

What is in this story?

Listen and say 🎧

ball

bear

toy

Download the audio at www.collins.co.uk/839681

cow

book

cat

Walk and hop.

Look at the shop.

4

Look at that!

It is a cat!

Walk and hop.
Look at the shop.

Oh, wow!
It is a cow!

Walk and hop.
Look at the shop.

Look, a bear!
On the chair!

Walk and hop.

Look at the shop.

Oh, look again!
It is a pen!

Walk and hop.
Look at the shop.

Is it a toy?
No, it is a boy!

Walk and hop.
Look at the shop.

Stop and look.
It is a book!

Walk and hop.
Look at the shop.

Oops, don't fall!
I see a ball!

Walk and hop.

Look at the shop.

What do you see?
I see me!

Walk and hop.

Look at the shop.

Look, come!
I see Mum!

Picture dictionary

Listen and repeat

chair

fall

hop

pen

shop

walk

After reading

1 Look and order the story

2 Listen and say

Collins

Published by Collins
An imprint of HarperCollins*Publishers*
Westerhill Road
Bishopbriggs
Glasgow
G64 2QT

HarperCollins*Publishers*
1st Floor, Watermarque Building
Ringsend Road
Dublin 4
Ireland

William Collins' dream of knowledge for all began with the publication of his first book in 1819.

A self-educated mill worker, he not only enriched millions of lives, but also founded a flourishing publishing house. Today, staying true to this spirit, Collins books are packed with inspiration, innovation and practical expertise. They place you at the centre of a world of possibility and give you exactly what you need to explore it.

© HarperCollins*Publishers* Limited 2020

10 9 8 7 6 5 4 3 2

ISBN 978-0-00-839681-7

Collins® and COBUILD® are registered trademarks of HarperCollins*Publishers* Limited

www.collins.co.uk/elt

British Library Cataloguing in Publication Data

A catalogue record for this publication is available from the British Library.

Author: Mary Roulston
Illustrator: Helen Flook (Beehive)
Series editor: Rebecca Adlard
Commissioning editor: Zoë Clarke
Publishing manager: Lisa Todd
Product managers: Jennifer Hall and Caroline Green
In-house editor: Alma Puts Keren
Project manager: Emily Hooton
Editor: Emma Wilkinson
Proofreaders: Natalie Murray and Michael Lamb
Cover designer: Kevin Robbins
Typesetter: 2Hoots Publishing Services Ltd
Audio produced by id audio, London
Reading guide author: Emma Wilkinson
Production controller: Rachel Weaver
Printed and bound by: GPS Group, Slovenia

MIX
Paper from
responsible sources

FSC
www.fsc.org

FSC™ C007454

This book is produced from independently certified FSC™ paper to ensure responsible forest management.

For more information visit: **www.harpercollins.co.uk/green**

Download the audio for this book and a reading guide for parents and teachers at www.collins.co.uk/839681